For Maureen Poland—M. W.

To Bill and Irene—J. C.

ISBN 0-439-68310-6

12 11 10 9 8 7 6 5 4 3 2 1   4 5 6 7 8 9/0

Printed in Singapore

First Scholastic printing, November 2004

The text for this book is set in Golden Cockerel.
The illustrations for this book are rendered in acrylics.

ROOM *for a* LITTLE ONE

A CHRISTMAS TALE

Martin Waddell

Illustrated by Jason Cockcroft

SCHOLASTIC INC.

New York Toronto London Auckland Sydney
Mexico City New Delhi Hong Kong Buenos Aires

It was a cold winter's night.
Kind Ox lay in his stable,
close to the side of the inn.

Old Dog came by.

He stopped and looked into the stable.

"I need somewhere to rest," said Old Dog.

"Come inside," Kind Ox said.

"There's always room for a little one here."

Old Dog came in and lay down in the straw.

He nestled close to Kind Ox,

sharing the warmth of his stable.

Stray Cat peered in.

She saw Old Dog and she stopped.

Stray Cat arched her back and her fur bristled.

"I'll not chase you," said Old Dog.

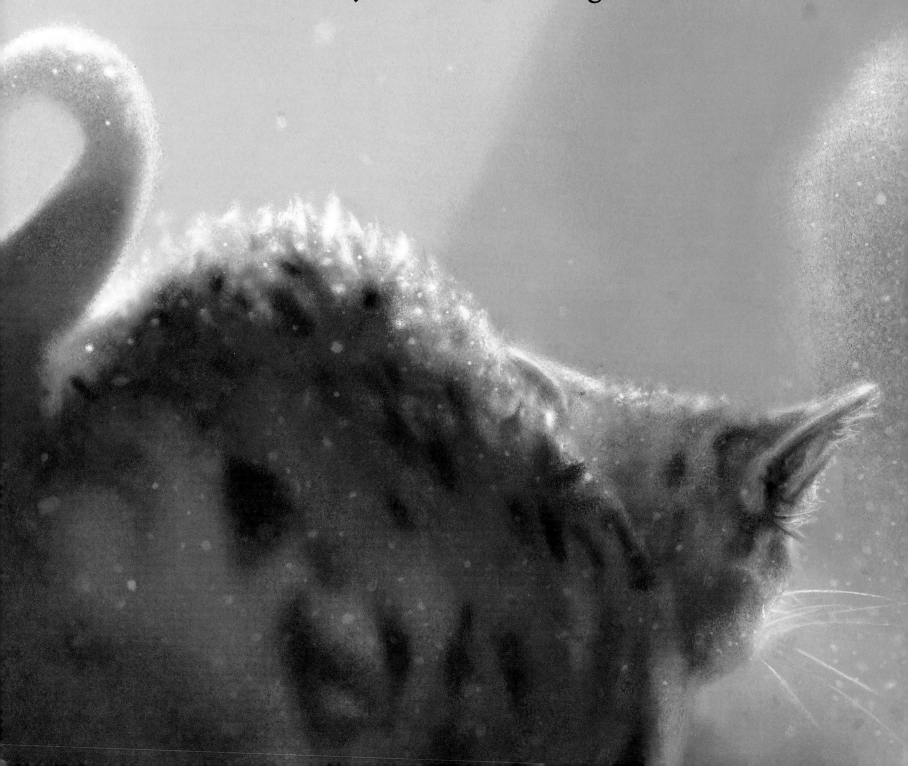

"Come inside," Kind Ox said.

"There's always room for a little one here."

Stray Cat came into the stable.
She curled up in the straw,
close to the friends she had found,
purring and twitching her tail.

Small Mouse stopped at the door of the stable.

She saw Stray Cat and she quivered with fear.

"You're safe here—I won't harm you," said Stray Cat.

"Come inside," Kind Ox said.

"There's always room for a little one here."

Small Mouse scurried in.

She nestled down warm in the straw,

in the peace of the stable.

Then Tired Donkey came.

Joseph led him along.

Mary rode on Tired Donkey's back.

Joseph was cold and Mary was weary,

but there was no room at the inn.

"Where will my baby be born?" Mary asked.

"Come inside," Kind Ox called to Tired Donkey.

"There's always room for a little one here."

Tired Donkey brought Mary into the stable.

Joseph made her a warm bed in the straw,

to save her from the cold of the night.

And so Jesus was born with the animals around Him;

Kind Ox,

Old Dog,

Stray Cat,

Small Mouse,

and Tired Donkey

all welcomed Him to the
warmth of their stable.

That cold winter's night,
beneath the star's light . . .

. . . a Little One came for the world.